Dedicated with love to every single child in Cordelia's class.
Thank you for your wonderful ideas, beautiful pictures for scenery,
and, most of all, your friendship.
And also a big thank you to Glenda Pleasants who contributed
so much to the making of this story.

This book was photographed in
Cordelia Castillo's class at Central Park East School
in the Jackie Robinson Educational Complex,
East Harlem, New York City.

Eddy's Dream

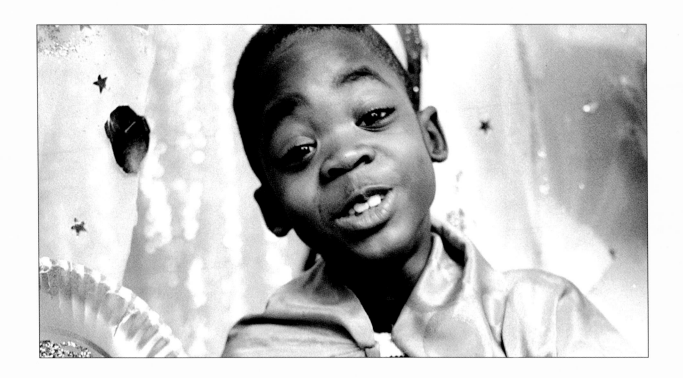

By Miriam Cohen
Photographs by Adam Cohen

Star Bright Books
New York

Published by Star Bright Books, Inc., New York.

Library of Congress Cataloging in Publication Data:

Cohen, Miriam.
    Eddy's dream / by Miriam Cohen; photographs by Adam Cohen.
        p.   cm.
    Summary : A group of children help one of their classmates stop spoiling their play and follow his own dreams.
    ISBN 1-887734-57-0
    [1. Schools Fiction.   2. Behavior Fiction.   3. Dreams Fiction.
4. Imagination Fiction.]   I. Cohen, Adam, 1954-   ill. II. Title.
PZ7.C6628Eg   1999
[E]--dc21   99-38636
                                                                              CIP

Manufactured in China 0 9 8 7 6 5 4 3 2 1

Michael wrote a story about his dream.

Everybody in first grade started to tell about their dreams.

But Eddy said,
"Dreams are stupid."

Trisha said, "I always dream that I am a ballet-dancing girl."

Shawn said, "I'm going to be an airplane pilot. That's my dream."

"My dream is if I would win the Lotto. I'd buy the whole Macy's store for my mother. And then I'd move it on our block," said Jerry.

"Why don't you make up a play about your dreams?" their teacher said.
"Yes! Yes!" the kids cried. Everybody except Eddy.

The kids fixed the curtain for
their theater.

"I am the DREAM MASTER!"
said Federico. "Get a costume. . .
the play is beginning!"

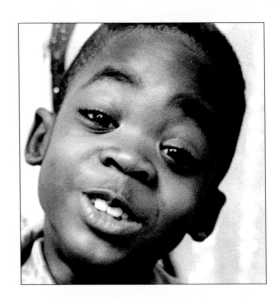

"DREAM MASTER! Ha, ha!"
laughed Eddy.

Eddy laughed at Michael and Shawn and Trisha.
"You look stupid in those costumes."

Federico called, "Anyone who wants to dream, go inside the curtain!"
"Come on, Eddy," said Shamika.

"Uh, uh. Not ME!" Eddy said.

Joseph said, "I'm putting stars and moons everywhere.
I'm making it like the sky, because that's where dreams come from."

The kids cried, "I'm first! Let me do it! I want to go first!"
Federico pointed with his sword. "Stand in a line! Trisha goes first."

"I'm dreaming. . . I'm dancing all over the stars," said Trisha.
"She's crazy!" Eddy said. "She's just standing right there!"

Eddy said, "This is so stupid!"

"All right, you can't be in the play," the kids told him.

"I don't want to be!" said Eddy. But he put on a costume anyway.

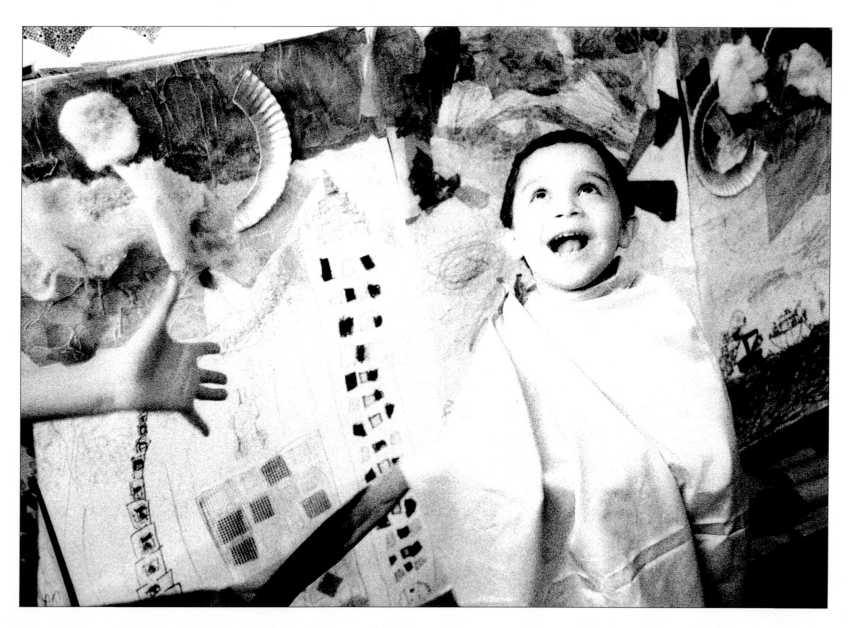

"It's Joseph's turn."
"I see my dog that's in heaven! He's back into a puppy again, and we're playing."

Shawn was telling a joke. But Federico said, "We have to work on our play!
It's Shamika's turn. Go in, Shamika."

"I dreamed I was famous. Everybody on my block said, 'Honey, you're gorgeous'."

"Ha, ha!" laughed Eddy.

"You better stop that or I'll punch you," Shamika told him.

Shawn was joking, "I dreamed that I turned everything in the world into gold. I'd be rich!"
"Then you wouldn't have any food," said Jerry.
"Yes I would, because I'd save some in a giant refrigerator."

"Dumb, dumb, dumb," laughed Eddy.

"Eddy is always laughing at us," said Shawn. "He is ruining our play!"

"I know why he's doing it," said Trisha. "I know EDDY'S DREAM!"

"No you don't!" shouted Eddy. "I'm not listening!"

"He's sad," Trisha said. "He always says he's going to see his Grandma in Puerto Rico.
But he never goes."

"Hey!" Shawn told the kids. "We could fly Eddy to see his Grandma in Puerto Rico. Line up the chairs into the airplane!"

"OK, everybody get in our airplane! Hold on! We're going up, " Federico said.
"This is so dumb," said Eddy. But he sat on one of the chairs.

Shawn threw glitter into the air. "It's beautiful!" the kids cried.

"Ooh, the stars are falling all over us!"

Shawn shouted, "Here we are in Puerto Rico!"

Eddy ran to the picture of Puerto Rico on the wall.
"Here's me and all my aunts and cousins and uncles. And my Grandma!
We're having a picnic with chicken and rice, and three kinds of soda!"

"My Grandma says, 'That boy is getting *so* big and handsome!' "

Their teacher peeked through the curtain and said, "It's time for math."

The kids shouted, "We're not here! We're in Puerto Rico with Eddy and his Grandma."

"Come back soon," the teacher said.

"We will. In just a little while."

Miriam Cohen has been writing books for children since 1967. Her first book, *Will I Have a Friend?* remains a favorite, and along with many of her 27 other books, is being read to children by parents who loved her books when they were young.

Miriam is an avid champion of children's emotional rights, and her sensitivity to their hopes, fears, and aspirations enables her to look at the world through their eyes. She understands their immense vulnerability and knows the importance of allowing children to develop naturally while at the same time encouraging and nurturing them.

Miriam has spent many hours in classrooms listening and talking to children. There she inhales their words and feelings and through her writing, speaks so directly to them that children see themselves in her books. *Eddy's Dream* is the culmination of her experience at Central Park East School in New York City.

Adam Cohen is Miriam Cohen's eldest son—one of three—all of whom were the inspiration for her first book. Adam is an award winning film maker and photographer. His photographs for *Eddy's Dream* are the result of months of collaboration with Miriam listening and watching the children shown in the book.